THE GHOST
OF CASTLE
McDUCKULA

Adapted by Maureen Spurgeon from
original Cosgrove Hall Productions
script by Brian Trueman
and directed by Chris Randall.

D1422709

CARNIVAL

Carnival
An imprint of the Children's Division
of the Collins Publishing Group
8 Grafton Street, London W1X 3LA

Published by Carnival 1988

ISBN 0 00 194474 6

Printed & bound in Great Britain by
PURNELL BOOK PRODUCTION LIMITED
A MEMBER OF BPCC plc

To the magnificent purple-clad highlands of Bonnie Scotland, there came one day an evil which before had never been known outside Transylvania, land of the most fearful and most terrible of all vampires . . .

It all began on a lonely, mountain road, a voice coming out of the mists . . .

"What a place to get a flat tyre!" groaned Count Duckula, standing back from his trailer impatiently "You going to be much longer, Igor?"

"Sir, I am doing my best!" Igor replied huffily. Mending cars, he considered, was not a suitable occupation for the manservant to the latest in a long line of vampire ducks. "These tools leave a lot to be desired."

"Well, it's lucky we had Nanny to use as a jack! You all right, Nanny?"

"Fine, Master Duckula!" replied Nanny from underneath the trailer. "But, who's this jack you keep talking about?"

Count Duckula and Igor pretended they hadn't heard.

"Well," said Igor at last, straightening up as best he could, "that's all I can do! But I expect it will break down again in a couple of miles . . ."

Duckula gave a snort.

"Oh, don't be such a misery, Igor! We'll never get to the Glensparrows Hotel at this rate!"

"Yes, Sir." Igor answered frostily. "You can come out now, Nanny!"

"Really, Milord," Igor continued, still looking rather peeved, "I do wish we had come by Castle Duckula, as usual!"

"The castle's due for service, Igor!" Duckula reminded him. "Besides, all my monster detecting gear is built into this trailer . . ."

"Oh, dear . . ." broke in Nanny in a quavering tone. "I'll never get supper ready with all this junk around, Master Duckula!"

"Junk!" echoed Duckula, most indignant. "*Junk?* Nanny, that's my monster monitoring equipment, in order that I, Count Duckula of Transylvania, can prove the existence of the Loch Ness Monster!"

"Really, Sir!" scoffed Igor from behind the wheel. "How a vampire duck of your breeding can believe in that story . . ."

"Just keep your eye on the road, Igor!" ordered Duckula, taking out an impressive-looking brochure. "Wow, I can't wait to get to this Glensparrows Hotel! Four poster beds . . . a jacuzzi . . . putting green . . . See that you polish my golf clubs, Igor!"

"Very good, Milord . . ." Igor replied, a secret smile fleeting across his gloomy face. What, he wondered, would Count Duckula say if he knew that he, Igor, was taking him not to Glensparrows Hotel, but to Castle McDuckula, home of his vampire relative, Rory McDuckula, the scourge of the glens . . .

"Are you sure this is the Glensparrows Hotel, Igor?" Duckula enquired some time later. "It doesn't look anything like the brochure!"

"Well, Sir," Igor responded, "you know what these travel firms are like . . ."

"Hmmm . . ." pondered Duckula, looking up at the towers of Castle McDuckula. He did not seem entirely convinced. "All right, then. Nanny can stable the werewolf!"

"I shall bring your bags in, Milord," said Igor, turning to unpack the luggage. "Would you like . . ."

"Ho'd on! Ho'd on!" barked a deafening voice, and a fearsome figure in a kilt and a tam o'shanter emerged from the castle. "Where are ye frae?"

Count Duckula at once turned to Igor, pointing an accusing finger.

"I knew you'd taken the wrong turning, Igor! We're in Siberia!"

"That, Milord, is a Scots accent. And I think you will find, Sir, that he merely wishes to know where we are from!"

"Aye!" barked the man. "Where are ye frae?"

Igor decided it was time for some formal introductions. So he stepped forward most politely, and made a bow.

"This is Count Duckula of Transylvania," he said, with deep respect. "And I am his manservant, Igor!"

"And, are you the Hotel Manager?" asked
Duckula.

"Bickering brattle!" came the snorted reply. "Lang
may your Sauchiehall Street!"

"Yes . . ." replied Count Duckula. "Well, if you
don't mind, I'll just call you Jock!"

"Er, I wonder if I might have a word with you," Igor
put in hastily, taking the stranger aside before he had
time to protest.

The two men spoke in a series of whispers, so Count
Duckula couldn't actually hear what they said . . .
apart that is, from a few words, such as: Duckula . . .
nephew's nephew's son's son . . . Glensparrows
Hotel . . . pretend . . . Manager . . ." – and none of
that made much sense to him.

It seemed to make the Hotel Manager laugh,
though . . .

"A fearfully refined good day to your lordship!" he greeted Count Duckula. "Terribly honoured that you have come to stay at our humble wee hotel!"

"Great Scot!" burst out Duckula, then felt himself going red. "Oh, sorry! Igor, I understood almost every word just then!"

"Aye, you'll soon get the hang of it, Sir," the Manager assured him. "Allow me to show you to your rooms!"

"Bring the bags, will you, Nanny!" Duckula yelled outside.

"Right you are, Master Duckula" came the reply – closely followed by a series of loud creaks, and then the splintering of wood!

"No, Nanny!" groaned Duckula. "Take them out of the trailer, first!"

"Ooops!" Nanny giggled. "Silly old me!"

There seemed to be a few more problems in store as soon as Duckula set eyes on the bedroom.

"I thought there was supposed to be a four poster!" he declared, looking all around.

"Aye," nodded the Manager. "This *is* one of our famous four poster bedrooms . . ."

"B-but . . ." spluttered Duckula. "The bed's not a four poster!"

"But the bedroom is, Sir! Look! A poster on each wall!"

Count Duckula tapped a webbed-foot with increasing impatience.

"And what about the whirlpool bath – the jacuzzi?"

"Well, there's a wash-basin there, with a stainless steel egg-whisk . . ."

Duckula suddenly saw red.

"All right, forget the jacuzzi! We'll just unpack and dress for dinner!"

"Very good, Sir," said the Manager, quite unperturbed. "Thank you, Sir . . ."

There was some improvement in the dining room, Count Duckula considered, admiring the heavy drapes and huge, stout furniture – rather like his own Castle Duckula, he thought, and began to wonder what there might be for dinner.

At last, he could bear the empty table no longer.

"Er – waiting for the other guests are we?" he enquired.

"Other guests?" repeated the Manager with a high-pitched laugh. "There are no other guests, Sir!"

"Hello . . ." came a voice which sounded rather familiar. "Hel-lo . . .!"

"That's fearfully good, Count Duckula!" cried the Manager. "I never saw your beak move!"

"That's because I didn't say anything!" snapped Duckula, feeling hungrier than ever.

"Anybotty at home der is?" continued the voice, and the door opened to reveal none other than Doctor Von Goosewing, the noted vampire catcher! "Dis is der Ruritania Guest House, ya?"

"No! This is Castle McDuck . . ." The Manager gave a hurried cough. "Ahem! It's the – er – Glensparrows Hotel!"

Von Goosewing was understandably confused.

"A first class room I had booked – und anudder fifth class for Heinrich, here . . ."

"I see," said the Manager. "So you need one room for you and one for Mr. Here!"

"Und one for Heinrich . . ." added Von Goosewing eagerly.

"Three rooms?" queried the Manager.

"Nein!" roared Von Goosewing.

"Nine rooms?"

"Two rooms!"

"So, who's sharing?"

"Who's caring?" demanded Goosewing, and Duckula raised his eyes in despair. Whenever bumbling old Goosewing came in, chaos usually followed . . .

But, this time, something else followed, too. Or, was it – someone? Anyway, it was a funny sort of see-through grey colour and was wearing an Elizabethan ruff.

"Excuse me . . ." the grey figure began, "Am I right for the Tower of London?"

"Fancy dress!" exclaimed Von Goosewing excitedly, scrambling for his camera. "Fancy dat! Of dis, a photograph I must have!"

"The Tower of London's four hundred miles away!" said Duckula, turning to the latest guest and ignoring Goosewing, as usual.

"Tut! I knew I should never have listened to Shakespeare!" The ghost scolded himself. "Good job I know a short cut!"

"Er – yes . . ." said Duckula, rather surprised to see the figure walking towards the wall. "Good-bye, then!"

"Good-day to you . . . ouch!" Even Duckula felt the bump. "I seem to have lost my touch . . ."

"You – er seem to have lost your head, as well!" commented Duckula.

And those were the truest words which Count Duckula ever spoke. Because, before his very eyes, the strange visitor was removing his head from his shoulders and giving the bump a comforting rub!

"Will somebody show the old fool where the door is?" stormed the Manager. "He's always doing that!"

"Most kind . . . most kind . . ." murmured the ghost, as Duckula led him on his way – still with his head under his arm. "Never used to bother with doors! Can't understand it . . ."

Maybe having a detachable head had something to do with it, Duckula considered privately. Next minute, there was a second crash – this time, into the door – and another loud "Ouch!" before the handle was finally turned.

"Oh, dear, oh dear!" the ghost trembled. "Whatever will Cromwell think?"

"Hamburgers und frankfurters!" Von Goosewing burst out, holding up his camera. "Somesink funny here is goink on!"

"Well . . ." Duckula hesitated, his wide eyes still on the door. "Not very funny . . ."

"On der picture, nuddings out is comink!" Goosewing went on, frantically waving the blank photograph under Duckula's nose. "Because, he a vampire was! Ja?"

"Well, no . . . It's because . . ." Duckula was sure Goosewing must have left the lens cap on.

But Von Goosewing was in no mood to listen to anyone.

"I show you! Anudder picture of mine host I am taking!"

"Oh, great!" cried the Manager, looking pleased for once. "I'd love a wee photy of myself!"

"Und here it comes!" exclaimed Goosewing. "Out of mine camera and . . . aaaagh! Blank, it is! You are a vampire, too!"

"Oh, well," replied the Manager. "Everybody knows that . . ."

"Don't humour him!" pleaded Duckula, still not guessing that the Manager was really his dreaded vampire relative, Rory McDuckula. "He's serious!"

"Ja, und now you vill perish!" yelled Von Goosewing. "Heinrich!" he called out. "Bring ze vampire blaster, quick!"

"Heinrich!" Goosewing yelled again. "Why is he never around when I want him? Now you shtay vere you are, you willain!"

"Och, aye!" answered McDuckula. "I'm willin'!"

"Condemned from his own beak!" screeched Von Goosewing, now in a real frenzy "Henrich! Heinrich!"

"I like that wee fellow!" said McDuckula, as Goosewing's cries faded into the distance. "He's the only one who's ever believed I'm a vampire!"

Duckula wasn't sure whether this was meant to be a joke, or not. So, he decided to forget it, and enjoy himself on the golf course instead.

"Well done, Milord!" cried Igor, applauding Duckula's very first shot. "Right on the green!"

"Yoo-hoo!" came Nanny's usual cry. "Master Duckula, your ball nearly went down a hole!

"Lucky I seen that little danger flag!" Nanny prattled on, handing over the ball. "I just managed to save it!"

"Drop it, Nanny . . ." warned Igor.

"Drop it? Well, if you say so, Mister Igor . . ."

"Ooooch!" Igor became the second one with a bump on his head that morning. "Nanny!"

Duckula felt he could bear it no longer.

"All right, all right! I'll play the shot from here! Give me an iron, Nanny!"

There was only one sort of iron which Nanny had actually heard of . . . So, off she bustled to the Castle McDuckula laundry room. Duckula was still holding out his hand by the time she got back.

"And about time, too . . ." he began. Too bad the iron was still hot!

"Yow-ooooh . . .!" screamed Duckula, dropping the iron without thinking – right on Igor's foot!

"Yow-ooooh . . .!" screamed Igor in accompaniment, and Nanny seemed quite affronted.

"Oh," she said. "We *are* in a mood today!"

"Nanny!" Duckula yelled, almost seeing blood red. "You silly old hen!"

"Oooh!" Nanny gasped indignantly. "You won't play at all if you carry on like this!" And, to prove her point, she snatched the golf club away!

"Nanny . . ." snarled Duckula between gritted beak. "Give me the club . . ."

"Not until you say you're sorry!"

"Allow me, Sir . . ." broke in Igor. "Nanny, the club! Let me have it!"

"Are you sure, Mister Igor?"

"Yes, Nanny," Igor responded soberly. "I am sure . . ."

"I'm not going to look!" Count Duckula told himself, turning away hurriedly with his hands over his ears. "I'm not going to look!"

There was a swish of the golf club, then a dull thud – and Igor lay groaning on the ground, suffering with the most terrible headache. Nanny was very surprised . . .

"Look at Mister Igor!" she said shakily, holding tight to Count Duckula's golf club with one podgy hand. "He's dropped off!"

Duckula let out a weary sigh.

"Come on, Nanny . . . Better get him up the wooden hill to Bedfordshire!"

If Count Duckula had been a true vampire like Rory McDuckula, then perhaps he would have noticed the deadly smell of garlic drifting towards them from the direction of Von Goosewing's bedroom . . .

"Zo!" Goosewing was muttering to himself, putting the finishing touches to a very strange combination of deer's antlers and a set of bagpipes. "Now I have made ein vampire blaster! Just fill the bag of der pipes mit garlic juice, und – fire!"

He punched hard into the bag. Nothing happened.
"Nuddings?" he murmured, squinting hard down one of the pipes to see if there was some sort of blockage. And sure enough, there was! As Von Goosewing discovered when the bagpipes gave a deep, mournful, jerky-sort of wail, and a whole bag of garlic fumes blasted him in the face!

"Ha! Zo!" cried Goosewing, delighted to find that his vampire catcher actually worked. "Good job I'm no vampire or quite giddy it might haf made me! Now, der vicious vampire iz . . ."

But, even as he spoke, the floor seemed to be spinning beneath his flapping, clumsy feet, and he fell to the ground with a sickening thud. Poor old Goosewing!

As for Igor, he was hardly doing much better. True, he lay on a sofa with Duckula bathing his forehead, but he was still a very worried manservant.

"Where's Nanny?" he kept saying, looking up at his young master with glazed eyes. "She isn't here, is she, Milord?"

"Now, now, Igor!" Count Duckula comforted him. "It's all right!"

"You – you won't let her hit me again, Sir – will you?"

"The lady's outside in the grounds, Mister Igor!" added Rory McDuckula. "She's practising for the Highland Games!"

"Oh, no . . .!" moaned Igor, closing his eyes and raising a bony hand to his throbbing head. "No!"

"Now, Igor," said Duckula, sounding much too cheerful, "don't worry! She can't hurt you here! Hang on, and I'll get you another aspirin!"

And he hurried towards the door – just a split second before a caber splintered its way through the ceiling, and landed on Igor . . . of course . . .

"I don't think I'd bother about aspirins," advised McDuckula. "He's nodded off again!"

"So, he has . . ." Count Duckula agreed. "Er – was that a sort of thumping on the wall? And – and a sort of, of . . ."

"Ooo--ooo--ooh!"

"There it is again!" shrieked Duckula. "What was it?"

"I say!" someone – or something – was calling out. "I say . . ."

"Try the door!" growled McDuckula, fast losing patience.

"Never mind, dear!" Duckula heard Nanny saying. "Just follow me!"

Suddenly, the wall bulged, then crashed in – leaving a hole large enough for Nanny to enter the room in her usual way, followed by the ghost.

"Ah, I could do that when I was younger!" he sighed ruefully. "I don't remember all the clouds of dust, though . . ."

"Ooh, hello, Master Duckula!" greeted Nanny. "You haven't seen a bit of a stick, have you?"

" If you mean a caber, Nanny," Duckula replied, "poor old Igor tried to head the flipping thing!"

Nanny received this piece of news with an air of scorn.

"Tut-tut! Silly thing! First he wants me to hit him with a golf club, then he tries nodding this 'ere caber! Must be going soft in the head!"

"Anyway," she gabbled on, stuffing the caber under her one good arm, "I'll get back to me practice, now!"

"Aye!" Rory McDuckula shouted after her. "And mind you close the wall behind you when you go out!"

"Oooh!" Nanny giggled. "Silly!"

Only a feeble-sounding groan broke the awkward silence, making both Duckula and Rory McDuckula rush to the sofa.

"Igor!" Duckula cried in concern. "Are you all right? Would you like another aspirin?"

"The last one seems to have made my headache worse!" moaned Igor with feeling. "All I need is a little peace and quiet . . ."

He started groaning again, raising a hand to his forehead once again. The smell of garlic had become quite overpowering . . .

"Zo!" roared Von Goosewing, bursting into the room with his vampire-blaster and aiming it straight at Rory McDuckula. "Your reign of terror is at an end!"

"And what's that you've got there?" McDuckula enquired, interested despite himself.

"Dis is mine own vampire blaster, and wit it, you I am going to blast!"

"Quick, Rory!" croaked Igor from the sofa. "Bite his neck!"

"Too late!" bellowed Doctor Von Goosewing. "Loaded with garlic ist mine vampire blaster, und to let you haff it, I am goink!"

Count Duckula had gone quite pale.

"Rory . . .? Vampire . . .? This can't be the Glensparrows Hotel, Igor! Come on, let's get out of here!"

" Come on, Igor!" Duckula shouted again, hurriedly squeezing Nanny into the trailer. "We're going!"

"After them in that balloon of yours, Von Goosewing!" screeched McDuckula. "They have no paid the bill!"

Count Duckula's trailer was already speeding along the mountain road – but Von Goosewing's balloon soon began gaining on them, urged on by Rory McDuckula, and the Tower of London ghost.

"Faster, Igor, Faster!" yelled Duckula.

"Going faster is no problem, Sir. Our brakes have failed!"

"They're getting away!" roared Rory McDuckula, eyes bulging at the sight of Duckula's trailer careering downhill. "Descend! Descend!"

By now, Duckula was near to panic.

"Look, Igor!" he shouted. "There's a lake at the bottom of this hill!"

"Loch Ness, Sir," declared Igor, with a brief glance at the guidebook. "You were anxious to visit it, I believe?"

"Yes, but not drown in it!" screamed Duckula in terror. "Igor, do something! Goosewing's still on our tail!"

And, so he was – heading straight onto a jagged finger of rock which tore into the balloon. Away it tossed and twirled in a hiss of hot air, losing height at an alarming rate as it darted down towards the water.

With a loud splash, Duckula's trailer plunged into the cold waters of Loch Ness, only seconds before Von Goosewing's deflated balloon. It was something of a shock when they found themselves coming up for air together!

Rory McDuckula was the first to speak, glaring at Duckula.

"You owe me four pounds, fifty pence!"

"And you, McDuckula," Goosewing joined in, "owe me four pounds for hire of balloon!"

"What about my equipment?" wailed Duckula.

"Suppose we've got another puncture?" croaked Nanny, remembering about being a car jack.

"Nanny . . ." Igor broke in. "Do go and make us some tea . . ."

None of them heard other voices in the cold, thin mist . . . voices which came from strange-looking heads on long necks, rising slowly out of the water . . .

"Look," cried the Loch Ness Monster. "A vampire duck!"

His brother gave a monsterish sort of rumbling chuckle.

"Simply your imagination!" he said.